The KNIGHT and the DRAGON

STORY AND PICTURES BY
TOMIE dePAOLA

G.P. PUTNAM'S SONS
NEW YORK

For all my friends in Red Wing

Library of Congress Cataloging-in-Publication Data
dePaola, Tomie. The knight and the dragon
Summary: A knight who has never fought a dragon and
an equally inexperienced dragon prepare to meet each other in battle.
[1. Knights and knighthood—Fiction. 2. Dragons—Fiction.]
I. Title PZ7.D439Kn [E] 79-18131
ISBN 0-399-20707-4
30

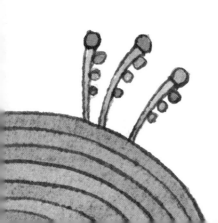

Once upon a time, there was a knight in a castle who had never fought a dragon.

And in a cave not too far away was a dragon who had never fought a knight.

One day the knight went to the castle library and took out
all of the books he could find on dragon fighting.

Meanwhile, back at the cave, the dragon had rummaged through all the things from his ancestors and found some books on knight fighting.

The knight began to build some armor.

The dragon practiced swishing his tail.

Meanwhile, back at the castle...

Meanwhile, back at the cave...

Finally, the knight and the dragon were both ready.
They sent each other a letter and set a time for...

the fight.